The Sleepover Club

Lauren. S.

*Have you been
invited to all these
sleepovers?*

Sleepover in Spain

by Narinder Dhami

Collins
An imprint of HarperCollins*Publishers*

The Sleepover Club ® is a registered trademark
of HarperCollins*Publishers* Ltd

First published in Great Britain by Collins in 1998
Collins is an imprint of HarperCollins*Publishers* Ltd
77-85 Fulham Palace Road, Hammersmith, London, W6 8JB

1 3 5 7 9 8 6 4 2

ISBN 0 00 675395 7

The author asserts the moral right to
be identified as the author of the work.

Printed and bound in Great Britain by
Caledonian International Book Manufacturing Ltd,
Glasgow G64

Sleepover Kit List

1. Sleeping bag
2. Pillow
3. Pyjamas or a nightdress
4. Slippers
5. Toothbrush, toothpaste, soap etc
6. Towel
7. Teddy
8. A creepy story
9. Food for the plane journey
10. A torch
11. Hairbrush
12. Hair things like a bobble or hairband, if you need them
13. Clean knickers and socks
14. Sleepover diary and membership card

PLUS: sun cream and sunglasses!!

CHAPTER ONE

Hiya, I'm back! It's me, Frankie, remember? I thought it was about time we had a chat 'cos it's been *ages* since I last talked to you. And I've got *loads* to tell you.

You haven't forgotten us, have you? There's me and my best mate Kenny, and Fliss and Rosie and Lyndz – the Sleepover Club. We've been having sleepovers for months now, and we always have a great laugh. So we were a bit shocked when Kenny said what she did. I mean, you know Kenny – she likes to stir things a bit. But this time what she said *really* made us sit up.

Anyway, it all started one afternoon at school. We were making models of horses out of clay (after our horsey sleepover, we're all nuts about horses now), so, of course, there was clay everywhere. Even Fliss was covered in it, and she's the neatest person in the known universe. She even gets her mum to iron her knickers!

"Hey, look!" Kenny stuck a lump of clay on the end of her nose, and grinned at the rest of us. "Pinocchio!"

"Thanks a lot, Kenny!" Fliss snapped, yanking it off her. "That's supposed to be my horse's tail!"

"All right, how about this then?" Kenny started sticking tiny bits of clay all over her face. "Look, it's Emma Hughes!"

We all fell about laughing. Emma's been off school with chickenpox, so her best mate Emily Berryman's had to hang out with dozy Alana 'Banana' Palmer instead. You remember Emma and Emily, otherwise known as the M&Ms, don't you? They're our Number One Enemies. Alana Banana's sort of our enemy too, but she hasn't got any brains so we don't worry about her that much.

"OK," I said, squinting down at my model. "Be honest, you lot. I can take it. Does this look like a horse to you or not?"

"Nope," said Lyndz.

"No way," said Fliss.

"No chance," Rosie added.

"It looks more like a giraffe," Kenny remarked.

"Oh, great," I said crossly, crushing my model flat. "Don't hold back, will you?"

"Your horse looks like it's been run over by a steamroller, Frankie," Mrs Weaver said, coming towards us. She raised her eyebrows at the squashed heap of clay in front of me. "What have you been doing for the last hour?"

"Sorry, Miss," I said quickly. "I just couldn't get it right." As my grandma always says, if at first you don't succeed – give up.

Mrs Weaver glanced at the clock. "Well, you've got about ten seconds left before we tidy up, so it's not worth starting again." Then she looked at us. We were all wearing overalls, but our hands were caked in clay, plus Lyndz had some in her hair and Kenny still had bits stuck on her face. "I think you'd better go and clean yourselves up too."

We lobbed our leftover clay into the clay bin, and ran for the sink in the corner. Fliss got there first.

"Ow! Stop pushing!" she complained, as we all tried to elbow our way in front of her.

"Hurry up or I'll shove a lump of clay down your neck!" Kenny warned.

Fliss jumped round, looking alarmed, and Kenny dodged smartly in front of her and began washing her hands.

"Oh, very funny!" Fliss sniffed.

"At least it wasn't ice cubes this time!" I pointed out, and we all cracked up, even Fliss. We hadn't forgotten about the sleepover when we'd tried to make a crazy video to send to *You've Been Framed*. It certainly starred the Sleepover Club, but not *quite* the way we had intended! The oldies hadn't forgotten it either, they *still* went on about it sometimes.

"So what exciting plans have you got for the sleepover at yours tonight, Rosie?" Lyndz asked.

"Well, I thought we could have a fashion show," Rosie suggested eagerly.

And that's when Kenny dropped her bombshell.

"Bor-*ing*!" she said immediately. The rest of us are really into clothes, but Kenny thinks dressing up means wearing her Leicester City football strip. With boots. "Can't we do something else?"

"Like what?" Rosie asked, looking offended. You know how prickly she can be sometimes.

Kenny shrugged. "I dunno... Something *different*. We always seem to do the same old things at sleepovers these days."

We all stared at her with our mouths open.

"Are you saying our sleepovers are *no fun* any more?" Fliss gasped, outraged.

"Nah, 'course not!" Kenny reached for a

paper towel. "Sleepovers are still *cool*! It'd just be even cooler if we did something different sometimes."

"Like what?" I asked. "And don't say we could play football."

"Well, why not?" Kenny said, and the rest of us groaned loudly. "OK, but what about having a sleepover somewhere else? We only ever go to each other's houses."

"What's wrong with coming to my house tonight?" Rosie began indignantly.

"Nothing, Rosie-posie!" Kenny interrupted, flicking some water at her. It was a great shot. It hit Rosie right in the eye, and she squealed. "But don't you remember what a brilliant time we had when we slept over at the museum?"

We had to admit, she had a point.

"Well, what did you have in mind?" I asked. "A sleepover in Sainsbury's, or what?"

"Ha ha, very funny, Francesca," Kenny began, trying to annoy me by using my full name, but right at that moment Mrs Weaver yelled over the noise: "Everyone in their seats now, please! I've got something very important to tell you."

We all scuttled back to our seats in silence. Kenny's remark had kind of thrown everyone, including me. *Did* we always do the same things at our sleepovers? Well, maybe we did, but we still had a great time. At least, I thought we did… No, I *knew* we did. If Kenny found them boring, it was *her* problem.

Mrs Weaver was waiting impatiently, glaring at Ryan Scott and Danny McCloud who were still chucking bits of clay at each other.

"Right, I want to tell you about a rather exciting trip that the school has arranged for this year group," she said, picking up a pile of papers from her desk. "And I have a letter for you to take home to your parents explaining all about it."

Nobody looked very thrilled. Have you ever noticed that what teachers think is exciting and what *we* think is exciting are never the same thing?

"The trip will be to the Costa Brava in

Spain for one week," Mrs Weaver went on.

There was a moment's breathless silence, and then the whole classroom erupted.

"A trip to *Spain!*" Fliss squealed. "That'll be brilliant!"

"I'm going!" Kenny said in a determined voice. "I don't care what I have to do to get my parents to say yes. I'll even be nice to Molly the Monster, sister from Hell, if I have to!"

"I reckon my mum'll let me go." Lyndz beamed all over her face. "Are you up for it, Frankie?"

"Are you kidding?" I gasped. My mum and dad are really boring when it comes to holidays. All we ever do is go to Scotland, or visit my gran in Nottingham or my grandad in Wales. Really interesting and exotic – not! "I've never been abroad before, and I really want to go!"

Suddenly Kenny bounced out of her seat with excitement. "Hey, we'll be able to have a sleepover in Spain! That'll be even *more* cool than the sleepover at the museum!"

Well, that just about did it. We were

almost wetting ourselves with excitement. Well, not quite all of us. Rosie wasn't looking very thrilled. In fact, she'd turned a funny pea-green colour.

"What's biting you, Rosie?" I asked.

"Kenny, will you sit down, please!" Mrs Weaver called. "And be quiet, everyone, so I can give you some more information about the trip before the home bell."

We all stared hard at Rosie, but we didn't get a chance to find out what the problem was because Mrs Weaver was giving us one of her looks.

"We're lucky because we've managed to book places at a very special holiday complex," she continued. "It has a swimming pool, all the usual activities, and it's right on the Costa Brava coast near the beach. But what makes this place different is that it's also an exchange centre where school children can come from all over Europe to meet each other..."

Mrs Weaver went droning on about how this was a great chance for us to make friends with kids from other European countries and learn all about each other's cultures and languages etc, etc, but nobody was listening. We were all too busy grinning at each other and making thumbs-up signs. It sounded totally brilliant. Spain, sun, sea, sand and the Sleepover Club! It was an ace combination. So I just couldn't understand why Rosie looked like someone was forcing her to spend a wet weekend in Birmingham with the M&Ms.

"Unfortunately, places are strictly limited, and only fifteen of you will be able to go." Mrs Weaver added, handing round the letters as the bell rang. "So if you're interested, you'd better bring your consent forms and the deposit to me first thing on Monday morning. Have a good weekend."

"What about you, Rosie?" Fliss asked anxiously as we picked up our bags. "You *are* going to come, aren't you?"

"'*Course* she is!" Kenny interrupted, flinging her arm round Rosie's shoulders. "We can't have a sleepover in Spain unless we're all there, can we?"

Rosie looked even more miserable. "I don't think I'll be able to. There's no way my mum can afford it."

We glanced at each other in horror. It just wouldn't be the same if we didn't *all* go.

"Well, what about your dad?" Kenny suggested. "You're always moaning about how he keeps going off on holiday with his girlfriend, even though he's promised to take you. I bet he'd be willing to pay for it."

"I don't want to ask him," Rosie muttered, and she turned and hurried out of the classroom before any of us could stop her.

"Well, that's going to ruin everything," I said angrily. Of course, the rest of us could still go, but we wouldn't be able to have a proper sleepover without Rosie, would we?

"Maybe we can talk her into asking her dad at the sleepover tonight," Lyndz suggested, and we all nodded. We had to do something, and fast, otherwise our dream of a sleepover in Spain would be over before it had even started.

CHAPTER TWO

"Mum!" I yelled as soon as I got home. "Can I go to Spain?"

My mum was working on the computer in her study, and she raised her eyebrows as I charged in, waving the letter.

"Did you say *Spain*, Frankie?"

"Yeah, there's a school trip to the Costa Brava!" I gave her the letter, and hopped impatiently from one foot to the other while she read it. "So, can I go?"

"Well, it does look quite interesting," my mum said thoughtfully. "It says here you'll get the chance to meet other kids from all over Europe, and learn about each other's cultures."

"Yeah, yeah, yeah," I muttered. Bor-*ing*! That wasn't what I was interested in. "What d'you reckon then, Mum? Can I go?"

My mum looked at me over the top of her glasses. "I suppose so, if your dad agrees."

"*Yes*!" I gave her a big hug. "Thanks, Mum!"

"What about the others? Are they going too?"

"Yep." I didn't say anything about Rosie getting her knickers in a twist, because I was pretty sure we'd be able to talk her into asking her dad for the money.

"The poor old Spanish don't know what they're letting themselves in for," my mum remarked, turning back to the computer.

I rushed out into the hall, grabbed the phone and punched in Kenny's number. I'd be seeing her in an hour or two at Rosie's, but I couldn't wait that long to break my good news.

"Hello?"

It sounded like Kenny at the other end of the line, so I started singing loudly: "*Oh, this year I'm off to sunny Spain! Y viva España!*"

There was a moment's silence.

"I think it's Kenny you want to talk to," Molly the Monster said in a freezing tone. I heard her slam the receiver onto the table and stomp off down the hall. A few seconds later Kenny picked up the phone. She was killing herself laughing.

"What did you say to the Monster, Frankie? She's got a face on her like a sour lemon!"

"Guess what?" I yelled. "My mum says I can go on the school trip!"

"Cool!" Kenny shouted joyfully. "So can I! And Monster-Features is so green with jealousy, she looks like the Incredible Hulk! Ow! Get off me, Molly!"

I waited impatiently while Kenny and Molly had a fight at the other end of the line.

"Kenny!" I yelled at last. "Get off the phone, 'cos I want to ring Fliss!"

"I'll ring Lyndz then. Right, Molly, you're

20

dead!" And Kenny banged down the phone.

"Of *course* I'm going!" Fliss said when I got through to her. "And so's Lyndz, I just called her. Now get off the phone 'cos I want to ring Kenny."

While Fliss was calling Kenny, I phoned Lyndz.

"So we're all going!" Lyndz said, delighted. "Except Rosie…"

"Well, we'll just have to try and talk her into it when we go over tonight." I glanced up at the clock. "Oh, rats, I'm going to be late!"

"So am I!" said Lyndz. "See you soon!"

I raced upstairs and started chucking things into my sleepover bag. Usually I take ages packing my stuff, but tonight I was too excited to care. I couldn't believe that I was finally getting the chance to go abroad. Fliss was always going on about Tenerife and Florida and Lanzarote and all the places she'd been to, and the others had been on foreign holidays too, so sometimes I felt really left out.

"Toothbrush, diary, membership card, pyjamas, slippers," I was muttering under my breath, when my mum came in.

"Hold it right there, Frankie," she said. "Mrs Cartwright has just phoned. Rosie's not very well, so the sleepover's off."

"What?" I bounced off the bed and onto my feet. "But she was fine at school today!"

My mum shrugged and went out, leaving me feeling really suspicious. It was all just a bit too convenient that Rosie was ill when she knew we were probably going to spend the whole sleepover trying to persuade her to come to Spain with us. So I legged it downstairs and phoned Kenny.

"I know – it stinks!" Kenny said when I got through. "I bet there's nothing wrong with her. I just spoke to Fliss, and she thinks Rosie's faking it too."

"I don't get it," I said, puzzled. "What's her problem?"

"I don't know, but we're gonna find out!" Kenny said. "I reckon we should all go over there anyway, right now. Can you meet us in half an hour?"

Fliss lived the closest to Rosie, so we decided to meet at her house. The others were already there when my mum dropped me off, and we set off for Rosie's place immediately.

"I don't know why Rosie's being so weird about all this," Kenny grumbled. "Anyone'd think she didn't *want* to go to Spain!"

"There must be a reason why she doesn't want to ask her dad for the money," Lyndz pointed out. "Poor old Rosie, I feel—"

"Really sorry for her!" we all chimed in.

"We won't be able to have a proper sleepover in Spain if Rosie doesn't come," Fliss said gloomily, as we went up to the Cartwrights' front door.

"She'll come," Kenny said confidently, ringing the doorbell. "Even if we have to carry her onto the plane ourselves!"

"I really want to learn flamenco dancing," I remarked. "Do you think we'll get a chance to have a go while we're there?"

"That'd be cool!" said Fliss. "I love those

big swirly dresses the Spanish dancers wear."

"Isn't flamenco dancing difficult?" Lyndz asked.

"Get out of it!" Kenny scoffed. "All you do is clap your hands and move your feet around a bit – like this." She started clapping her hands and stamping her feet and twirling round in circles, shouting "*Olé!*"

"Watch it, Kenny!" Fliss said, looking alarmed as she twirled faster.

Kenny suddenly got dizzy, staggered and pitched head-first into one of the bushy shrubs near the front door. That cracked us all up. She was still picking leaves out of her hair when Rosie's mum opened the door.

"Oh – hello!" she said, looking dead surprised to see us. "I wasn't expecting you."

"We thought we'd come and see how Rosie is," I explained.

"Yeah, we want to find out if she can come on the school trip to Spain," Kenny said eagerly. "*We're* all going."

"Oh?" Mrs Cartwright looked surprised.

"She hasn't mentioned it to me. But if she wants to go, I'm sure her dad will be happy to pay for her."

We all looked at each other. No problem there then. So why was Rosie being so funny about it all? It was a real mystery.

"Rosie's in bed, so go right up." Mrs Cartwright ushered us in. "She's got a bad headache, so don't make too much noise, will you?"

We all went up the stairs, trying not to make too much of a racket, but it wasn't easy because there was no carpet down. Rosie's house is brilliant – it's big and it has loads of rooms, but it's in a right old state. Her dad, who's a builder, had bought the house and started doing it up, but then he'd left and gone to live with his girlfriend. He was still *supposed* to be fixing the place up, but he hadn't got very far. Rosie was always moaning about it.

We stopped outside Rosie's bedroom door, and I knocked gently. No answer.

"Maybe she's asleep," Lyndz whispered.

"No chance," Kenny snorted. "We *know* there's nothing wrong with her!" And she flung the door open.

Rosie didn't see us at first. She was dancing round the room in her teddy-bear pyjamas with a Walkman in her hand and headphones over her ears, pretending to be Posh Spice.

We all waited in the doorway with our arms folded until, eventually, Rosie turned round. When she saw us, she nearly dropped down dead with shock.

"Wh– what're you doing here?" she squeaked, pulling the headphones off.

"We've come to see our sick friend," Kenny said with heavy sarcasm. "Where is she, by the way?"

Rosie blushed. "All right," she muttered sheepishly. "I'm not really ill."

"*Big* fat hairy surprise!" Kenny snapped. "So what's going on then?"

Rosie looked down at her pink furry slippers. "I didn't want to have the sleepover because I didn't want you going on at me all night about coming to Spain."

"But what's the problem?" I asked with a frown. "Your mum says that your dad'll pay."

Rosie went even redder. "I– I– I've never been on an aeroplane before!" she stammered. "And I'm scared!"

"Is that all!" Kenny began, then shut up as I elbowed her in the ribs.

"But you said you'd been abroad!" Fliss pointed out, looking puzzled.

"We went on the ferry," Rosie mumbled miserably, "and I wasn't too keen on *that*."

"I've never been on a plane before either, Rosie," I reassured her. "So I'll probably be wetting myself too. Don't worry about it."

"And I've only done it once," Lyndz chimed in. "It's really not so bad."

"I hate the take-off, though," Fliss said with a shiver. "You know, that bit when the plane first gets off the ground and it's really noisy and you feel like you're going to be sick—"

Kenny, Lyndz and I all glared at her.

"But otherwise it's brilliant, honestly,"

Fliss said quickly.

Rosie was starting to look a bit more cheerful.

"I do want to come, really," she admitted. "I'm just nervous, that's all."

"Me and Lyndz will hold your hand," I told her. "And if you throw up, we'll throw up too, just so you don't feel embarrassed."

Rosie began to giggle. "Well, I'd better go and ring my dad then, hadn't I?"

"*Yes!*" Kenny jumped up and punched the air. "The Sleepover Club's going to Spain!"

CHAPTER THREE

"*Zanahoria*," I said, checking my Spanish dictionary again. "What d'you think that means?"

The others groaned. We were sitting on the plane, waiting to take off for the Costa Brava, along with the rest of the kids who were going. Me and Lyndz were sitting with Rosie, to give her moral support, and Kenny and Fliss were across from us. Everyone was so excited, we were totally hyper, and we were driving Mrs Weaver and Miss Simpson, the other teacher who was going with us, crazy. At the moment they were running up and down the aisle, checking that nobody had been left behind in the duty-free shop.

"Frankie, you've been driving us bananas with that dictionary for weeks now!" Kenny glared at me. "Give it a rest, will you!"

"Come on, don't be a dweeb!" I retorted. "We've got to make a bit of an effort to learn some of the language."

"Why?" Fliss asked, fastening her seat belt. "Loads of people in Spain speak English anyway."

"That's not the *point*," I sighed. "Go on, have a guess what *zanahoria* means."

"School?" Rosie suggested.

"Aeroplane?" Lyndz offered.

"An annoying twit who won't keep their big mouth shut?" Kenny asked pointedly.

"Ha ha. No, it's Spanish for carrot."

"Oh, great big fat hairy deal," Kenny retorted. "That'll be so-o-o useful."

Rosie was rummaging in the pocket on the back of the seat in front of her.

"What's this for?" she asked, holding up a paper bag.

"What do *you* think?" Kenny grinned.

"You mean they give you a *bag*?" Rosie looked horrified at the thought. "That's really embarrassing!"

"It'd be even more embarrassing if you *didn't* have one!" Fliss pointed out, and we all started giggling.

"OK," I said, flipping through my dictionary again. "Try this one. *Conejo*."

"Haven't a clue," Lyndz yawned.

"No idea," said Rosie.

"Rabbit!" I said triumphantly.

"Oh, radical," said Kenny. "So if I happen to meet a talking *conejo* on the Costa Brava, I can ask him if he wants a *zanahoria*."

"All right, girls?" Mrs Weaver stopped at our seats, looking about ten million times more stressed out than she usually does at school. "Now, are you sure you've got all your hand luggage with you?"

"Yes, Miss," we chorused. We all had our Sleepover Kit in our hand luggage, including our diaries and membership cards. Our diaries contain our biggest and most intimate sleepover secrets, so there was no way we wanted to lose *those* in a hurry.

"Good. Now I want you to be on your best behaviour at all times," Mrs Weaver went on. We could tell that she was warming up to the speech she'd given us nearly every day at school for the last few weeks. "Just remember that you're representing Great Britain while you're in Spain, and we want people to get a good impression, not only of our country, but also of our school…"

We all tried not to yawn. Kenny was pretending to listen, but she'd secretly pulled out a can of Coke from her pocket, and was trying to open it without Mrs Weaver noticing.

"…so be aware that at all times you are an ambassador for our country—

"Aargh!" Mrs Weaver screamed, and we all ducked as Kenny popped open the can, sending a shower of Coke everywhere.

"Sorry, Miss!" Kenny spluttered. "It must have got shaken up!"

Mrs Weaver looked as if she'd quite like to

grab Kenny and give *her* a good shaking.

"Just remember what I've been saying, Laura," she remarked in a threatening tone, and went off, wiping her face.

"Wow, she called me Laura!" Kenny said, passing the can round. "That means she's *really* mad."

"Now she's telling Ryan Scott off," Lyndz said. "Did you see that ginormous bar of chocolate he bought in the duty-free shop? Well, he's eaten half of it already!"

"Better lend him our sick bags," Kenny remarked. "I suppose you're well pleased Ryan's coming with us, aren't you, Fliss?"

Fliss blushed. She's had a thing about Ryan Scott for ages.

"Well, at least he's better than the M&Ms!" she retorted.

We all grinned at each other. The M&Ms were missing out on the trip because Emma Hughes had been absent when the forms were given out. Emily Berryman didn't want to go without Emma, so we were only stuck with Alana Banana. And as I said before, she doesn't really count.

Suddenly the plane started to move, and I sat up. "We're off!"

All the kids from our school cheered and started giving each other high fives as the plane taxied towards the runway. Lyndz was trying to cheer and drink Coke at the same time, so, of course, she got hiccups, and then one of the stewardesses had to bring her a glass of water.

"What's happening now?" Rosie asked nervously as a voice over the speakers told us to watch the stewardesses' demonstration carefully.

"They're going to tell us what to do if the plane goes down," Kenny said through a mouthful of chocolate.

"What!" Rosie turned pale.

"Don't get all wound up," I told her, as the nearest stewardess showed us how to put on a life jacket. "We'll be fine."

The plane came briefly to a halt at the top of the runway. There was a great roar of engines, and Rosie closed her eyes as it picked up speed.

"I want to go home," she muttered.

The plane rushed forward and then, just when we were beginning to think that it would never make it, it lifted up into the air, climbing higher and higher every minute.

"Hey, that wasn't so bad!" Rosie said, relieved. She leant across Lyndz, who was sitting by the window, and looked down. "Wow! Look at the airport, Frankie – it looks really small already."

I didn't answer. I was slumped in my seat with my eyes closed, shivering all over, and feeling as if I'd left my stomach behind on the ground when we took off.

"Hey, Frankie," Kenny called across the aisle, "what's Spanish for 'airsick'?"

"Shut it, Kenny," I muttered, feeling my tummy do five backflips in a row as the plane carried on climbing.

Even though I began to feel better when we were right up above the clouds, once you couldn't see the ground the journey was actually pretty boring. The only good bit was when the stewardesses brought round some food, but even compared to Sleepover Club standards of cooking, it didn't taste that great. It seemed ages until the Captain finally told us that we were coming in to land at the Spanish airport.

"We're here! We're here!" Rosie exclaimed, bouncing up and down in her seat.

"Hey, take it easy," I said, alarmed. "You don't want to rock the plane while we're landing!"

The others started to laugh.

"What's Spanish for 'dumbo', Frankie?" Fliss asked between giggles, and I chucked the dictionary at her.

Coming down was loads better than going up, and when I stepped off the aeroplane, I couldn't believe that I was actually in Spain. It was dark, so we couldn't see much, but although the air felt warmer than at home, the airport didn't look that different from the one we'd just left behind in England.

We had to wait ages to collect our bags, and Kenny got told off by Mrs Weaver for trying to ride round on the luggage carousel, then at last we all piled out of the airport and onto a minibus. But I felt a bit let down *again* because there was nothing new to see on the journey, either. Just some roads, and loads of cars.

"This is no different from Leicester!" I said in a disappointed voice to Fliss.

"I've never seen a palm tree in Leicester!" Fliss pointed out.

"OK, *except* for the palm trees."

Lyndz and Rosie fell asleep, and the rest of us could hardly keep our eyes open either, but when we arrived at the holiday complex, we all sat up and had a good look.

It was *brilliant*. The place was floodlit, so we could see that all round the grounds were blocks of dormitories where we'd be sleeping, and in the middle of them was a huge swimming pool with two water-slides and a chute, which was surrounded by loads of deck chairs. There was also a games hall, tennis courts, a bowling alley and a kind of mini funfair. Our eyes were out on stalks.

"This is *fab*!" Kenny gasped, as we all practically fell over each other in our rush to get off the coach. "We're going to have a brilliant time!"

We'd pulled up outside one of the dormitory blocks, right next to where another coach was already parked. A load of kids who looked as if they were Spanish were just climbing off and waiting for their suitcases and bags.

"Right, gather round, please," Mrs Weaver called, waving her clipboard at us as our driver started to unload the luggage. "I'm going to tell you your room numbers, so listen carefully. Lyndsey Collins, Rosie Cartwright and Felicity Sidebotham – number seven. Francesca Thomas, Laura McKenzie and Alana Palmer – number twelve..."

"We're not in the same room!" Rosie gasped, looking worried. "How're we going to have a sleepover if we're not all sleeping together?"

"Kenny and me'll just have to sneak into your room," I said.

"But we're in with dozy Alana Banana!" Kenny groaned.

"Don't worry about Alana, we'll just ignore her like we usually do—" I began. But Kenny wasn't listening.

"Hey, that girl's nicked my bag!" she yelled. And the next second she was legging it over to one of the Spanish kids who'd been waiting beside the other coach. I followed her. The girl, who was wearing a Real Madrid football shirt, was walking into the dormitory block with four other girls, and she was carrying Kenny's blue Adidas bag.

"Kenny! What on earth's going on?" Mrs Weaver hurried over as Kenny tried to yank the bag out of the girl's hands.

"That's my bag, Miss!" Kenny gasped. She was having a tug-of-war with the Spanish girl, who wouldn't let go either.

"No, it is not!" the girl snapped, glaring at Kenny. "This bag is mine!"

39

"Give it back!" Kenny pulled even harder.

"Er – Kenny…" Fliss hurried over to us. She had a blue Adidas bag in her hand. "I think you'll find *this* one's yours. Our coach driver's just got it out of the boot."

"You'd better apologise, Kenny," Mrs Weaver said tartly, and went off.

"Sorry," Kenny muttered to the Spanish girl, who was giving her a dirty look. So were her four friends.

"It is OK," she snapped. "Everybody know the English is stupid!" She glanced at Kenny's Leicester City football shirt. "And the football teams are terrible!"

"What!" Kenny clenched her fists. The five girls giggled and went into the dormitory block, chattering to each other in Spanish.

We all glared after them.

"What a load of stuck-up nerds!" Rosie gasped.

"Yeah, they'd better keep out of our way in future!" Kenny said furiously

But d'you know what? I had a feeling we hadn't seen the last of those girls…

CHAPTER FOUR

"Oh, this is *ace*!" I gasped, as Kenny and I went out onto the balcony and looked across the holiday camp. Although it was still quite early in the morning, the sun was already warm and the sky was blue. We could even see the sea in the distance. At last I was starting to feel that I was actually in Spain.

"Fabbo," Kenny agreed, squinting in the bright light. "Hey, did you hear Alana Banana snoring last night? She sounded like a bullfrog!"

"Don't be unkind to bullfrogs!" I laughed.

"Come on, let's grab our stuff and go to the bathroom before she wakes up."

We tiptoed back into our room, which was really small and only just about had enough room for three beds and a wardrobe. Then we collected our towels and toothbrushes and legged it, leaving Alana Banana still snoring. We were at the other end of a long corridor from Fliss, Rosie and Lyndz, so we hurried down to their room and banged on the door. They were just getting out of bed.

"Come on, lazybones!" Kenny said, sticking her head round the door. "If we get washed and dressed quick, we can go out and explore!"

"Mrs Weaver said we weren't to go anywhere before breakfast—" Fliss began, but Kenny grabbed a pillow off Rosie's bed, and lobbed it at her.

"Oh, don't be such a goody-goody, Fliss! Come on!"

Two minutes later we were all in the bathroom. There was no one else there, so we each got a shower cubicle to ourselves.

"Does anyone know what we're doing today?" Kenny called over the noise of the running water.

"Mrs Weaver said that we're going to the beach!" Rosie called back.

"Sounds ace!" I said, grabbing my towel and drying myself off. "I hope we don't see those snooty Spanish girls again though."

"Well, if we do," Kenny said grimly, "I'm gonna tell them exactly what I think of them!"

"I thought Mrs Weaver said we were supposed to be making friends with kids from other countries," Fliss pointed out.

"Yeah, but not if they're snooty, stuck-up and a pain in the neck!" Kenny retorted.

We opened the doors of our showers, and came out. Then we stopped in our tracks. The five Spanish girls were standing there in their pyjamas, holding their towels and toothbrushes, glaring at us.

Kenny was the first to recover. "Got a problem?" she asked jauntily.

The girl who'd had the Adidas bag the night before stepped forward, looking furious. "Yes, I have. You."

"*Ten cuidado*, Maria," said the tallest girl, who had long black hair in a ponytail.

"Careful, Kenny," I said at almost exactly the same moment.

Kenny and Maria ignored both of us.

"Oh yeah?" Kenny moved forward too, staring Maria right in the eye. "Well, that's just your tough luck, isn't it?"

"Cool it, Kenny," I said firmly, grabbing her arm. "Let's get out of here." And between the four of us, we managed to get her outside into the corridor.

"What did you do that for?" Kenny said crossly. "I was just about to knock her block off!"

"That's what we were worried about!" Rosie pointed out. "D'you want Mrs Weaver to go ballistic?"

Kenny suddenly started grinning from ear to ear. "Hang on a sec," she whispered, and tiptoed back into the bathroom. The Spanish girls had already gone into the showers, and Kenny moved silently along the row until she saw Maria's red pyjamas, which were hanging over one of the doors. Kenny reached up, grabbed them and chucked them straight out of the open window.

"*Ay*! *Mi pijama*!" We heard Maria yell indignantly from inside the cubicle, but we didn't wait to see what happened. We fled along the corridor back to our rooms, laughing our heads off.

"That'll show her!" Kenny giggled, as we skidded to a halt outside Fliss, Rosie and Lyndz's room. "Serves her right!"

"I see you're all up bright and early." The door of the next room opened and Mrs Weaver came out. "Breakfast in ten minutes, remember."

"Hey, that's a bit of a downer," I whispered to the others as Mrs W went off. "I didn't know she was in the room next to you lot. If we have a sleepover, she'll hear everything!"

"Yeah, that's a point," Kenny agreed. "And we definitely can't have one in our room because of Alana Banana."

"Alana's so dopey, she might not notice," Lyndz said hopefully.

"Yeah, but we'd have to listen to her snoring!" I said. "Nope, we'll just have to have the sleepover in your room, and hope Mrs Weaver doesn't catch on."

"Come on, let's get dressed, and go and grab some breakfast." Kenny headed back down the corridor towards our room. "I'm starving!"

The canteen was in a large, spacious hall next door to our dormitory block. Most of the kids from our school were already there, sitting at long tables, and so were the teachers. We collected our cereal and toast, and joined them.

"Where's Alana, Frankie?" Mrs Weaver asked with a frown.

"She's just getting up, Miss," I replied. "Well, she'd opened her eyes anyway."

We sat down and started to attack our food hungrily.

"Right, everyone, we'll be meeting at the entrance of our dormitory block in exactly half an hour," Mrs Weaver said briskly. "We've got some very exciting activities planned for you down on the beach this morning, and you'll have a chance to meet up with some of the other school children who are staying here."

Kenny groaned. "Oh, great! Like I *really* want to spend the morning with those gruesome Spanish girls!"

"I wonder if Maria got her pyjamas back!" I said with a grin.

Just at that moment Maria and her friends walked into the canteen. They clocked us straightaway, but instead of looking angry, they started giggling and pointing at us.

"Hey, what's going on?" Fliss asked. "Why're they laughing at us?"

"Who knows?" Kenny shrugged. "Just ignore them."

We soon found out why Maria and her friends were in hysterics on our way back to the dormitory block. There was a tree just

47

outside the canteen, and there were clothes hanging off some of the branches. There was a football shirt, two T-shirts, a pair of jeans and a pair of pink knickers.

"That's my best top!" Lyndz wailed.

"Those're my favourite jeans!" I yelled.

"That's my Spice Girls T-shirt!" Rosie gasped.

"And those're my knickers!" Fliss hissed in a strangled voice.

"Someone's chucked our clothes up here!" Furious, Kenny jumped up and tried to grab her football shirt, but she couldn't reach it. "And I bet I know who!"

"What *I'd* like to know is how they knew where to find our stuff in the first place," I said.

"They must have watched which rooms we went to when we left the bathroom," said Lyndz.

"Hurry up!" Fliss begged, as Kenny shinned quickly up the tree. "Before anyone comes!"

"You know what?" Kenny said through

gritted teeth as she grabbed Fliss's knickers and chucked them down to her. "This means war!"

CHAPTER FIVE

"Look at them!" Kenny whispered in my ear, disgusted. "They're laughing their stupid heads off!"

"Yeah, we've got to think of a way to get our own back!" I agreed, and Rosie, Fliss and Lyndz nodded.

We were just getting onto our minibus and the Spanish girls were getting onto their one, which was parked next to it. They were smirking at us smugly through the windows.

"I'd like to push them into the swimming pool!" Fliss muttered under her breath as we sat down. "I can't believe they threw my knickers into a tree!"

"They're gonna be sorry they messed with us," Kenny growled. "I ripped my footy shirt while I was getting it down."

We all glared at the Spanish girls, and they pulled faces at us.

"Is there a problem, girls?" Mrs Weaver asked with a frown, as she got on the bus.

"No, Miss," we all said quickly.

"Well, I hope no one's forgotten their sun cream!" Mrs Weaver said with a smile, as the driver climbed in and we moved off. "We're going to be at the beach for most of the day."

"Oh, I can't wait to get to the sea!" Fliss squealed excitedly. "I'm going to lie in the sun and get a brilliant tan!"

"You'll be lucky," Kenny retorted. "Didn't you see that list of activities Mrs W had on her clipboard? We've got to choose one to do."

"What?" Fliss asked, looking dismayed.

"Yeah, volleyball, cricket, Frisbee, surfing." Kenny ticked them off on her fingers. "Oh, and five-a-side football."

"NO!" the rest of us said loudly.

"Oh, *all right*," Kenny grumbled. "But what about surfing? That looks pretty cool."

"Hey, Fliss!" Ryan Scott called from the back seat. "You haven't forgotten your *underwear*, have you?" And he and his mate Danny McCloud fell about laughing.

Fliss turned the colour of a ripe tomato. "I could kill those girls!" she muttered.

"Oh, let's forget about them and have a good time," Lyndz suggested cheerfully. "That's why we're here, remember?"

We all got more and more excited as the minibus headed out of the holiday complex, and down to the sea. As we drove through the town, we saw loads of cafés and restaurants, and all kinds of souvenir shops.

"I hope we get a chance to do some shopping," Rosie said. "I want to buy a donkey in a straw hat!"

"How gross!" Kenny remarked. "Hey, that'd be the perfect present for Molly the Monster!"

We all leapt out of our seats at the first

glimpse of the sea. As the minibus drew to a halt, my eyes were almost falling out of my head because I'd never seen a beach like this one. It was long and winding, the sand was clean and golden, and the water was a clear, deep green. It was a whole lot better than some of the grungy beaches I'd been to in England!

"Ace!" I said happily, as we all pulled off our shoes and followed Mrs Weaver across the sand. "I hope it's chucking it down with rain back home, and the M&Ms are getting soaked!"

"Talking of the M&Ms," Rosie said in a low voice, "they'd probably get on really well with *them*!"

We all looked down the beach. Maria and her friends were a little way off with the rest of the group of Spanish kids, standing round their teacher, Miss Moreno.

"They've got it coming!" Kenny muttered, giving them the evil eye. "Nobody ruins my footy shirt and gets away with it!"

"Oh, ignore them," I said. "We don't want

them spoiling our day!"

"Yeah, Frankie's right," Lyndz agreed. "Let's just keep away from them!"

Yeah, *right*. When Mrs Weaver asked us what activities we wanted to do, we decided on surfing, and she sent us over to our instructor, who was an Australian called Jo. Guess who was already standing there with surfboards in their hands?

"G'day, girls!" said Jo, who sounded like she ought to be in *Neighbours*. "Great to meet you all. This is Maria, and this is Pilar" – she pointed to the tallest girl – "And this is Isabella, and the twins Anna and Elena."

Isabella, Anna and Elena hadn't said much so far, but they were making up for that by staring at us extra-snootily. Isabella was small and thin and had long hair in a ponytail, and Anna and Elena were taller with short, dark curly hair, although for twins they didn't look that much alike.

"Well, we're going to have a ripper time this morning, girls," Jo said cheerfully, as Kenny pulled a cross-eyed face at Maria.

"And you're all going to be great mates at the end of it!"

We all stood there silently, eyeballing each other grimly.

"Er – let's get started then." Jo looked a bit flustered as she passed us each a surfboard. "Have any of you guys ever surfed before?"

"Yes," Pilar said immediately.

"No," I said, and the Spanish girls all started grinning.

"It's cool," Kenny cut in quickly. "We'll be able to do it, no probs."

"It's not quite as easy as it might look." Jo was beginning to get even more flustered as she spotted Maria sticking her tongue out at Kenny. "But the waves here are pretty gentle, so you'll be quite safe."

"They *would* be able to surf," I muttered to Fliss, as we took off our T-shirts and shorts. "Now we're going to look right idiots next to them."

"I know," Fliss began. Then she let out a scream. "Look!"

"What's up, Fliss?" Kenny asked. "Seen a

shark?"

"That – that Isabella's got the same swimsuit on as me!" Fliss spluttered.

We all looked at Isabella, who'd just taken her shorts off. She was wearing exactly the same hot-pink bikini with white spots on as Fliss was.

"I'm not wearing this again!" Fliss grumbled, stuffing her clothes into her beach bag.

"Could be embarrassing when you're sunbathing then," Kenny remarked.

"Don't be daft," Fliss retorted, "I've brought six other swimsuits with me!"

"All ready, girls?" Jo hurried over to us. "Let's go down to the water."

Maria, Pilar and the others had already waded out into the sea, and were lying on their fronts on their surfboards, riding in on the waves.

"Hey, that's not *proper* surfing!" Kenny scoffed. "You're supposed to stand up!"

"Yeah, we can do *that*, no problem!" Rosie agreed.

Just then a really big wave came in, and all five of the Spanish girls jumped upright on their surfboards, and rode the wave into the shore like experts. We all looked at each other in dismay.

"Right, put your boards down in the water, and lie on them," Jo instructed us. "The first thing we're going to practise is paddling out."

Jo showed us how to move ourselves into the water by paddling with our arms. Then we had to turn round on the boards so that we were facing the beach, and let the waves shoot us back in. It wasn't as easy as it looked. The first big wave sent me tumbling off my board, and under the water. When I came up spluttering, Rosie, Kenny, Fliss and Lyndz were all doing the same thing, and Maria and the others were killing themselves laughing, and calling out things in Spanish, which we couldn't understand.

"Go with the wave, don't try to fight it," Jo told us. "And when you feel confident, you can start moving the board around a bit, and try coming in at an angle."

After we'd been practising for a while, we started to get pretty good, so, of course, Kenny began to get a bit cocky.

"I'm gonna stand up for this one!" she yelled, as we saw a huge wave beginning to break.

"No, Kenny!" the rest of us screamed, but she ignored us. As the wave crashed down, she jumped up on her board – and disappeared completely. She reappeared a moment later, coughing and spluttering and looking half-drowned.

"Oi, Kenny!" Maria called, helpless with laughter. "You want to do this, yes?" And she stood up on her board and surfed into the shore.

"OK, that's it!" Kenny gasped, coughing up about ten pints of sea water. "It's payback time. They're gonna get what's coming to them right now!"

CHAPTER SIX

"What're we going to do?" Lyndz asked, as we paddled over to them.

"Watch me!" Kenny replied. She went right up to Maria, who didn't see her coming because she was swimming out to catch the next wave, and tipped her off her surfboard. We all screamed with laughter, and paddled off. Jo started calling us from the beach, but we ignored her.

"Aargh!"

We all heard Fliss scream, and turned round. We were just in time to see Isabella grab hold of Fliss's board, and tip her into the water with a splash.

"Right! You're dead!" Kenny yelled. "Come on, let's get them!"

We all paddled furiously towards the Spanish girls. Lyndz got there first, and pushed Elena right off her board, and Rosie lunged at Anna and tipped her off too. I headed for Pilar. I reckoned that was only fair, because she was the tallest, like I was. But I never got to her, because now Jo was *really* mad.

"STOP THAT AT ONCE!" she roared, wading out into the water. "AND GET BACK HERE RIGHT NOW!"

We all paddled sulkily back to the shore.

"What on *earth* do you think you were doing?" Jo shouted furiously at us. "You could have hurt each other!"

"That was the idea!" Kenny muttered.

After the battle of the surfboards, Jo sent us off in disgrace. Luckily Mrs Weaver didn't notice because she was teaching a group of kids to play volleyball, so we grabbed a spare Frisbee and messed about with that for a while. Then it was time for lunch.

"I reckon we got a result, anyway," Kenny said as we sat under a parasol, unpacking our sandwiches. "We knocked three of those nerds off their boards, and they only got Fliss."

"I just wish I'd got Pilar," I remarked, as I towelled my hair dry. "I reckon she's the leader of that gang, even though Maria's got the biggest mouth!"

Rosie's eyes widened. "Hey, that's just like you and Kenny!"

"What?" Kenny and I stared at her.

"Well, Pilar's really tall, and Maria likes football…" Rosie's voice trailed away.

"We're nothing *like* them!" Kenny said indignantly, and Rosie turned pink.

"I'm *not* surfing again this afternoon," Fliss said firmly. "I just want to lie here and get brown."

"I want to ring my mum," Rosie said.

"Get out of it!" Kenny scoffed. "We've only been here a day!"

"I know," Rosie looked a bit embarrassed,

"I just want to check how everyone is."

That started me thinking about my mum and dad and Pepsi, my dog, back home in Cuddington. Suddenly England seemed a very long way away.

"I haven't been away from home on my own this long before," Fliss muttered tearfully.

So there we were, munching our sandwiches, on a beautiful, hot day, watching the sea roll in, and looking like really sad cases. Even Kenny was looking a bit down. I decided it was time for some action.

"Hey, why don't we have our Spanish sleepover tonight?" I suggested.

"I thought we were going to wait till the end of the holiday," Lyndz said.

I shrugged. "So what? We can have more than one, can't we?"

Everyone nodded eagerly. Just thinking about having a sleepover made us all feel a lot more cheerful.

"We'll have to buy some food for the

midnight feast," Rosie pointed out.

"We can get that from the shop at the holiday complex, no problem," I said. "Kenny and me'll sneak over to your room tonight as soon as Alana Banana's asleep."

"What if she wakes up and sees you're gone?" Fliss asked anxiously.

Kenny shook her head. "She won't!" she said confidently. "Alana Banana's so dozy, she'd sleep through an earthquake!"

"Isn't she asleep yet?" Kenny whispered, leaning across the narrow gap between our beds, so that Alana wouldn't hear.

"Nope, I can still hear her moving around."

"She's a real pain in the neck!" Kenny groaned, flopping back onto her pillow. "Look, it's after midnight already!"

When we'd got back from the beach earlier that afternoon, we'd played tennis and gone bowling. We were both so wiped out from all the exercise and sea air, we could hardly keep our eyes open. Maybe arranging a sleepover for tonight hadn't been such a good idea…

"Ow! My nose is sore!" Kenny complained. "I think I've burnt it. Does it look red?"

"Yeah, it's glowing in the dark like Rudolf's," I told her.

"Oh, ha ha." Kenny said, then she went quiet. Somehow I managed to keep my eyes open, and as soon as I heard Alana Banana snoring, I reached over and poked Kenny.

"Ow! Wassat?" Kenny mumbled dozily.

"Alana Banana's asleep at last," I said, swinging my legs out of bed. "And so were you, by the sound of it!"

"No, I wasn't." Kenny rolled out of bed, yawning. "Come on, let's go. And don't forget the food."

I picked up the carrier bag. We'd had a Spanish thing called *tapas* for our dinner, which was brilliant. There were loads and loads of little dishes, all containing different things like olives, potato omelette, stuffed mushrooms, sausages and salads. So while we were eating we'd all been busy pocketing stuff that we could keep for our midnight feast.

We took our torches and tiptoed over to the door. Kenny pulled it open cautiously, and we looked out into the brightly-lit corridor.

"I'm going to turn the light off," Kenny whispered, "so we've got a better chance of getting away if either of the teachers hear us."

"Well, I hope we don't barge into Mrs Weaver's room by mistake!" I said anxiously. Mrs W had given us a long talk the night before about how we were not to sneak into each other's rooms at night under any circumstances. Of course, we weren't going to take any notice of *that*. We were just going to do our best not to get found out.

Kenny hurried across to the light switch on the opposite wall, and flipped it off. Immediately it went so dark, we couldn't make out our hands in front of our faces. We didn't have time to turn on our torches though, because the next moment the lights came back on.

Kenny, who was coming towards me, froze. "Someone's used one of the other switches!" she hissed. "Quick, shut the door – they might be coming this way!"

Kenny dashed back into our room, just as Pilar came round the corner. Quickly we pushed the door to, and waited, our hearts pounding. Then we looked out cautiously again, just in time to see her go into the bathroom.

"She must be going to the loo," Kenny whispered. "D'you think she saw us?"

"I don't think so." I pulled the door open. "Come on, we'd better get to the others before she comes back. Leave the light on this time, or she might get suspicious!"

We ran down the corridor to room number seven. But when I turned the handle, the door wouldn't budge.

"It won't open!" I gasped.

"What!" Kenny nearly had a fit. "They must've locked it on the inside! We'll have to knock."

"Don't be an idiot!" I hissed. "If we do that we'll wake up Mrs Weaver!"

"Well, what d'you suggest then? We've got to do *something*!" Kenny hissed back. "Pilar'll be out in a minute, and she'd just love to drop us right in it!"

Suddenly we heard the noise of a bolt being pulled back, and the door opened. Fliss was standing there, blinking at us sleepily, and we nearly knocked her over as we barged in. Rosie and Lyndz sat up in bed, yawning and rubbing their eyes.

"Sorry," Fliss said. "We fell asleep, and forgot we'd bolted the door."

"Thanks a bunch!" Kenny said. "We nearly got caught by Pilar. She's in the bathroom."

The others looked alarmed.

"Did she see you?" Rosie asked.

"Nope." Kenny shook her head. "Good job too, because she'd probably tell Mrs Weaver like a shot."

I got under the duvet at the bottom of Lyndz's bed, and Kenny got into Fliss's.

"What shall we do first?" Lyndz asked in

a low voice.

"Something quiet," Fliss begged. "I'll die if Mrs Weaver wakes up."

"We could write in our diaries," Rosie suggested. "That's pretty quiet."

"Good idea," I agreed.

"Yeah, OK, but we ought to do something *special* first," Kenny added.

"Like what?" Fliss frowned.

"Well, it's our first sleepover in a foreign country," Kenny explained, "so maybe we ought to make a speech or something."

I grinned. "Go on, then."

"OK." Kenny jumped out from under the duvet, and stood up on Fliss's bed. "Welcome to our very first *dormir sobre*!"

We all blinked.

"You what?" I said blankly.

"*Dormir sobre* – it's Spanish for sleep-over!" Kenny grinned. "I looked it up in Frankie's dictionary. Well, I looked up *sleep* and I looked up *over*, and then I just put them together!"

"Nice one!" Lyndz said, and we were all

going to applaud, but then we remembered Mrs Weaver was just next door, so luckily we didn't.

"You know what?" Kenny went on. "I reckon we should try to have a sleepover in every single country in the world – then we'd get into the *Guinness Book of Records*!"

"What, even Iceland?" Fliss shivered.

"Yeah, a sleepover in an igloo!" Rosie suggested, and we all put our hands over our mouths to stop the giggles.

We were still laughing when, without warning, the door flew open and Mrs Weaver stormed in.

CHAPTER SEVEN

Kenny was so shocked at the sight of Mrs Weaver, she fell backwards and landed on top of Fliss, who squealed.

"What on *earth* is going on in here?" Mrs Weaver said furiously, looking round at us with her worst, beady-eyed stare. "You were told not to leave your rooms at night unless you needed to go to the bathroom!"

"Yes, Miss. Sorry, Miss," we all said miserably.

Suddenly I noticed Pilar standing in the corridor, peeping in through the open door. She saw me looking at her, and grinned wickedly before walking off.

"I'm very disappointed with your behaviour," Mrs Weaver went on sternly, making us all feel about five centimetres tall. "These rules were made for a reason – we have to know exactly where everyone is in case there's a fire drill, or some other emergency."

We all sat there silently, not daring to say anything.

"Francesca and Laura, go back to your room immediately. We won't say anything more about this, but" – Mrs Weaver stared round at us, her face grim – "if it happens again, Miss Simpson and myself will have to move into the same rooms as you. Now off you go."

"That was close," Kenny muttered, as we hurried back to our room under the stern eye of Mrs Weaver. "I don't fancy bunking in with the teachers!"

"Yeah, well, maybe if Pilar hadn't dropped us in it, we'd have got away with it!" I said angrily.

Kenny's eyes widened. "You mean, Pilar *did* see us, and told Mrs Weaver?"

I nodded. "I reckon so. She was in the corridor when Mrs Weaver was bawling us out – didn't you see her?"

"No, I didn't!" Kenny clenched her fists. "The nasty little toad! Well, we'll just have to be more careful next time."

"What, you mean we're still going to try and have a sleepover?" I asked.

"'Course we are!" Kenny said in a determined voice as we entered our room, where Alana Banana was still snoring loudly. "We're not going to let Pilar and her gang get the better of us, are we?"

"Nope, I guess not," I replied. But I couldn't help wondering what Mrs Weaver would do if she caught us out of our room again at night.

"So Pilar *did* see you!" Rosie exclaimed, as we ate our breakfast the following morning.

"Yep, we reckon she dropped us right in it," Kenny said furiously, mashing her

Weetabix to a pulp. "So the question is, what're we gonna do about it?"

"Oh, never mind them," said Lyndz. "What are we going to do about our sleepover?"

"Well, I think we ought to wait a few days and then try again," Kenny said.

Fliss turned pale. "What if we get caught though? Mrs Weaver'll go completely ballistic."

"So?" Kenny shrugged. "What can she do? She can't put us in detention!"

"She could stop us going to the beach every day," Rosie pointed out.

"She could make us sit in our rooms and do schoolwork," Lyndz chimed in.

"She could send us home on the next plane," I added.

"Oh, and she could ban us from going on *any* other school trip *ever*," Fliss finished off.

"All right, all right," Kenny muttered, wrinkling her bright pink nose. "We'll just have to make sure we don't get caught then, won't we?"

As we went out of the canteen, Maria, Pilar, Isabella, Anna and Elena were just coming in, and they all grinned nastily at us.

"What a sad thing your teacher catch you last night!" Maria giggled, and then they all started talking in Spanish.

"It really bugs me when they do that!" Kenny said crossly, as we stalked past them with our noses in the air. "I wish I could understand what they're saying!"

"Well, I did try to teach you some Spanish, but you weren't interested!" I pointed out.

Kenny sighed. "I want to know how to say 'Shut up, you're totally getting on my nerves', *not* 'Do you want a carrot?'"

"What're we doing today?" Fliss asked. "Are we going to the beach again?"

"Yeah, but just for the morning," Rosie said. "It's free time, so we can do what we want."

"Excellent!" said Lyndz. "I reckon we should keep right away from those Spanish girls *and* from Mrs Weaver all day!"

We all thought that was a good idea, so

when we got to the beach, we bagged a couple of parasols as far away from everyone else as we could, and spread out our towels underneath them.

"I've got to keep my nose out of the sun," Kenny said, arranging herself so that the bottom half of her body was in the sun and her face was in the shade. "It's so red, it's glowing!"

"Yeah, you won't need to use your bedside lamp if you want to read at night!" I remarked, lying face down on my towel.

"Yee-argh!" I leapt up again as Kenny slapped some ice-cold sun cream on my back, and the others giggled. Although what had happened the night before had been a bit of a downer, we'd all cheered up again.

"I don't believe it!" Fliss suddenly screeched.

"What?" We all sat up.

"That Isabella's got the same swimsuit on as me *again*!" Fliss howled, looking outraged.

The Spanish girls were with their teacher

quite a way down the beach from us, but we could still see that Isabella was wearing the same costume as Fliss – a bright blue one-piece with pink flowers on it.

"It's not funny!" Fliss groaned as we tried not to laugh.

"Maybe you'd better go and ask her if she has loads of clothes, and likes fluffy toys!" Kenny said with a grin.

"And weddings!" Rosie added.

"She's nothing like me at all!" Fliss sniffed. She was starting to get wound up, so we dropped it.

After we'd sunbathed for a bit, we went down to the sea, and splashed around. We met up with some German girls who were staying at the holiday complex too, and they were brilliant. We didn't do any serious swimming because we felt too lazy, but we had a great time.

"I don't know why anyone goes on holiday in England when they could come here!" I sighed, floating on my back in the warm water. "If we were at home now, we'd be running in and out of the freezing sea, waiting for the rain to stop!"

"Hey, stop knocking England!" Rosie said. "It's not so bad."

"Yeah, we've got Walkers cheese and onion crisps!" Lyndz pointed out. "*And* Buckingham Palace!"

"We've got the best pop groups," Fliss joined in.

"And don't forget Leicester City FC!" Kenny added.

"OK, OK! I get your point, but you've got to admit, Spain's got better weather!" I dived under the water, and tried to grab Kenny's legs.

Kenny jumped out of my grasp. "Last one back to the parasols has to kiss Ryan Scott!" she yelled, and we all legged it out of the sea, and up the beach. Guess who was last.

"Oh, bad luck, Fliss," Kenny said sarcastically, as we waited for her to catch us up. "You lost."

Fliss turned pink, but then she frowned. "Hey, what's happened to my bag?"

All of Fliss's stuff was scattered across her towel, and her pink-and-white-striped beach bag was lying on its side.

"Hey, d'you think someone's been nicking our money?" Kenny gasped, grabbing her own bag.

Fliss, who was quickly going through her things, shook her head. "No, it's all here, my purse and everything. My bag must've just fallen over—" Then she stopped. "Hang on a minute. My sleepover diary's gone!"

"Are you sure?" Rosie asked, as Fliss rooted frantically through her belongings again.

"Certain sure!" Fliss said, tipping her bag upside-down and shaking it. "I know I put it in when I packed it this morning!"

We all searched the area around our parasols, picking up our towels and looking underneath, and checking our own bags, but the diary was nowhere to be seen.

Fliss was gradually turning as white as a ghost. "Where can it be?" she wailed. "I've got to get it back! It's got all our sleepover secrets in it!"

"Just a minute," Kenny said slowly, "you don't think *they've* nicked it, do you?"

"Who?" I asked, not realising for a second whom Kenny meant.

Kenny pointed down the beach at Maria and the others. "I reckon it's just the kind of thing they'd do! And they've had plenty of time while we were in the sea."

"I know they're pretty gross, but I don't think they'd go through our bags," Lyndz said doubtfully.

"Well, they wouldn't have to, would they?" Kenny pointed out triumphantly. "If Fliss's bag had fallen over and her stuff was lying there, all they'd have to do is pick the diary up!"

Fliss was now looking more green than white. "B– but there's everything about the Sleepover Club in there!" she stammered. "And – well…"

"What?" Kenny asked grimly. "Spit it out, Fliss."

"There's stuff about Mrs Weaver," Fliss

muttered, "*and* Ryan Scott."

"If they've nicked that diary, we'll be in heaps of trouble when they read it!" I said urgently. "We've got to find out if they've got it or not – and fast!"

CHAPTER EIGHT

"It's not here!" Fliss wailed, standing in the middle of the wrecked bedroom. We'd tipped out the entire contents of hers and Rosie's and Lyndz's bags, and we'd emptied the wardrobe. We'd even stripped the beds. But we hadn't found a sausage.

"What am I going to do?" Fliss moaned. "I'm dead if anyone reads that diary!"

"We're *all* dead," Kenny pointed out. "*Everyone's* going to know about our sleepovers."

"My membership card's tucked inside it too," Fliss muttered dismally.

"Oh, great, we might as well just invite everyone in the whole world to join the Sleepover Club!" Kenny said crossly. "We're not going to have any secrets left!"

"Cool it, Kenny!" I said as Fliss bit her lip, looking upset. "We still don't know where the diary is. Fliss might have dropped it somewhere."

"Yeah, but that means *anyone* could get their hands on it!" Lyndz said gloomily. "What if one of the kids from our school finds it?"

Fliss turned pale. "If Ryan Scott reads my diary, I'm going home on the next plane!"

"And what about Alana Banana?" Rosie said. "She might find it and keep it to show the M&Ms!"

We all looked at each other in silent horror. Things were going from bad to worse. We had to get that diary back or the Sleepover Club would be finished, and Fliss would die of embarrassment every time she saw Ryan Scott.

The sound of giggling behind us made us

turn round. Maria, Pilar and the others were standing in the corridor, laughing and pointing at us.

Kenny clenched her fists. "Right!" she announced. "I'm going to ask them straight out if they've got Fliss's diary, and if they have, I'm going to make them give it back!"

"Don't be an idiot, Kenny!" I hissed, grabbing her arm as she lunged forward. "If they *haven't* got it, they might go looking for it!"

Kenny stopped in mid-charge. "I hadn't thought of that."

"What do you look for?" Pilar called, as the other girls sniggered. "Something important?"

"Mind your own business!" Fliss snapped.

The Spanish girls went off, still laughing, and we all looked at one another.

"So d'you think they've got it or not?" Lyndz asked.

"I dunno," Kenny said with a frown, "but if they have, I bet they're going to make us sweat a bit before they give it back."

"Well, until we find the diary, everything's on hold," I said. "We can't have a sleepover in case they tell Mrs Weaver what we're planning. She'll go off her head if she catches us again."

We all looked gloomy.

"Well, I'm not sitting round here doing nothing!" Kenny raced over to the door.

"Where're you going?" Rosie asked, alarmed.

"To search their room!" And Kenny dashed off down the corridor.

"Kenny! Wait!" I yelled, but she ignored me.

"What's she playing at?" Fliss gasped, as we ran after her. "She'll be in big trouble if she gets caught!"

"The biggest," I said grimly, skidding to a halt outside the Spanish girls' room, just as Kenny closed the door behind her.

"What're you doing?" Rosie hissed, sticking her foot in it. "Get out of there!"

"I'm only going to have a quick look." Kenny hurried across the room, and started looking in the bedside lockers. "It's not like I'm going to *nick* anything."

"How come they've got a room for five people?" Fliss grumbled, looking round her. "If we had this room, we could have sleepovers every night!"

Suddenly Lyndz froze. "Someone's coming!" she hissed.

"Quick, under the beds!" Kenny ordered us.

We all flung ourselves down onto the carpet, and each rolled under one of the beds. Rosie rolled under the same one as me, so I had to shove her out of the way. She'd only just hidden herself under the next bed, when the door opened, and the Spanish girls came in.

We all lay there as still as statues, hardly daring to breathe. The girls were walking round the room, chatting in Spanish, and all I could see of them was their shoes. They kept coming right up to the beds, and then walking away again. At one point Maria's trainers were only about a millimetre from my nose.

Then, all of a sudden, they went out again and closed the door. I gave a sigh of relief, and rolled out from under the bed. The others did the same.

"Right, now we're getting out of here!" I said, glaring at Kenny and daring her to disagree.

"Oh, we might as well have a quick look now we're here—" Kenny began. But we didn't give her a chance to finish. We surrounded her, and frog-marched her out of the room.

"So what happens now?" Rosie asked, when we were safely outside.

"Not a lot," I said. "We can't do anything until we find that diary, so we'd better get looking."

We spent most of that afternoon searching for the diary around the holiday complex. The threat of those Spanish girls, or Mrs Weaver, or Alana Banana, or Ryan Scott getting hold of it was hanging over us all the time. It was a real downer because none of us could relax and enjoy ourselves until we knew where the diary was.

We didn't have a chance to look for it the following day, though, because our group, along with some of the German and Danish kids, went on a day trip to Barcelona. Pilar, Maria and the rest of their gruesome gang didn't come, so we got away from them for a while.

Barcelona was *excellent*. There were loads of interesting buildings, including a really weird-looking cathedral, a palace, big gardens and parks, a harbour, and streets and streets of interesting shops. We also saw a ginormous statue of Christopher Columbus, which had a lift inside so that you could ride right up to his head and look out over the whole city. We all wanted to go up it, until Mrs Weaver told us that about twenty years ago his head had fallen off! Then we weren't so keen.

We were taken to all the cultural places first, and then we were allowed to go shopping. That was the best bit! The shops were radical, and we all went mad and bought loads of stuff. Fliss and Rosie both got fans, and we all bought castanets, as well as presents for our families.

"That was ace!" Rosie sighed as we climbed back onto the minibus at the end of the day. "I love my castanets!"

As soon as we sat down, we all got our castanets out, and started clicking them and shouting "*Olé!*", until Mrs Weaver gave us a look from the front of the minibus.

"What's in that bag, Kenny?" Fliss asked curiously, pointing to a paper bag sticking out of Kenny's pocket.

Kenny put her hand in the bag, and pulled out a box of stinkbombs. We all stared at it.

"Where did you get those?" Lyndz asked.

"I nipped into a joke shop while you were looking at the fans." Kenny grinned. "I just thought they might come in handy."

"What for?" Fliss looked blank.

"Oh, get a life, Fliss!" Kenny said impatiently. "For those Spanish girls, of course. I reckon we should stinkbomb them every night until they give the diary back!"

We all started to laugh.

"Kenny, you're not serious!" I raised my eyebrows.

"'Course I am!" Kenny retorted. "I'm going to sneak down to their room tonight, and chuck a stinkbomb through their door!"

That wiped the smiles off our faces.

"You must be mad!" Fliss gasped. "It's miles too risky!"

"What if Mrs Weaver's on the prowl and catches you?" Rosie pointed out.

"It's not worth the hassle, Kenny," Lyndz advised her.

"Oh yes it is!" Kenny looked stubborn. "I'm well fed up with them taking the mickey out of us all the time, and I'm going to do something about it!"

"But they might not even have the diary!" Fliss wailed.

Kenny shrugged. "Who cares about the diary? I just wanna teach them a lesson!" She looked round at us. "So, are you coming with me? Or are you all a bunch of wimps?"

CHAPTER NINE

"Frankie!" Kenny leant over and shook my shoulder. I woke up with a start. "Time to go."

"OK," I said reluctantly, pushing back the duvet. We'd all tried to talk Kenny out of her crazy idea, but she wasn't having any of it. And we couldn't let her go on her own, could we? The Sleepover Club had to stick together, even though we would all be in deepest doom for the next million years if Mrs W caught us red-handed.

We went quietly over to the door. I was kind of wishing that Alana Banana would wake up, and then we wouldn't be able to go. But she was dead to the world, as usual, snoring like a foghorn.

Kenny turned off the corridor light, just to be on the safe side, and we tiptoed down to the others' room. It was pitch black without the lights on. We had our torches with us, but we didn't want to use them unless we had to, so we felt our way along the wall until we got to the right door.

"Here we are," Kenny whispered, her hand on the door handle. She flicked the torch on just to check, then quickly turned it off again. "Oh, rats, that's number eight – Mrs Weaver's room!"

"Oh, nice one, Kenny!" I groaned.

We hurried on to number seven. The others sat up in bed as we went in.

"All set?" Kenny asked breezily.

"Hang on a sec." Rosie leant over and picked something up off Fliss's bedside locker. "Guess what we've found!"

"Fliss's diary!" Kenny gasped. "Where was it?"

"Under my bed," Fliss muttered, looking highly embarrassed. "It must've fallen out of my bag."

"Oh, great!" I said crossly. "All that worrying for nothing!"

"So we don't have to go and let off the stinkbomb now, do we?" Lyndz pointed out, and I've got to admit, I felt pretty relieved.

"Are you *kidding*?" Kenny said fiercely. "They threw our clothes into that tree, remember? Anyway, I spent 300 pesetas on these stinkbombs, and I'm not going to waste them! Now, come on!"

Fliss, Rosie and Lyndz climbed out of bed reluctantly. They looked as nervous as I was feeling, but none of us was going to let Kenny down.

Kenny opened the door, and Fliss gave a little squeal.

"What's the matter?" Kenny hissed, alarmed.

"It's completely black out there!" Fliss muttered. "I'm going to get my torch."

Kenny grabbed her arm. "No, it's too

risky. We'll be safer in the dark."

"But how're we going to find our way?" Fliss wailed.

"We'll all stay in a line behind Frankie, and keep close to the wall," Kenny told her.

"Oh, great!" I grumbled. "Looks as though I'm in front again, as usual!"

We all got into a line – me at the front, followed by Kenny, Rosie, Lyndz and Fliss – and we linked hands. Then we shuffled out into the dark corridor.

Once we'd got past Mrs Weaver's room, we began to breathe more easily, but it was still a long way to the Spanish girls' room. I led everybody slowly down the corridor, feeling my way along the wall, until we came to the corner.

Suddenly, someone behind me hiccuped. Although it wasn't very loud, it *sounded* loud in the dead silence. My heart beating fit to bust, I yanked on Kenny's hand, and pulled everyone round the corner with me. We all flattened ourselves against the wall, and waited for the lights to go on. But nothing happened.

"Lyndz, you idiot!" I whispered. "Why didn't you hold your breath?"

"It wasn't me!" Lyndz whispered back indignantly.

"Well, who was it then?"

No one answered.

"Maybe this is going to be like a horror film," Kenny said, "and the monster'll join the end of the line and bump us off one by one."

"I'm not standing at the end then!" Fliss said, alarmed, trying to push in between Rosie and Lyndz.

"Ssh, we're here now anyway," I said.

Kenny flicked the torch on quickly to check that it was the right room, and then she crept across the corridor.

"Turn the torch off before you open the door!" I told her, but Kenny shook her head.

"I want to make sure I chuck the stinkbomb right into the middle of the room!" she said, taking the box out of her pyjama pocket.

94

We all watched breathlessly as Kenny opened the door, dimming the torch by putting her hand over the beam. *Then* we all nearly dropped down dead, as suddenly she flung the door wide open.

"What're you doing?" I gasped, my heart in my mouth.

"They're not here!" Kenny said crossly. "Look!"

She shone the torch round the room, and we all peered in. Every one of the beds was empty!

"Well, where are they then?" Rosie said, but we didn't get a chance to discuss it. Someone was opening the door of a room further down the corridor...

"Quick!" I hustled everyone into the room. "Get into the beds!"

We each dived into one of the empty beds, and lay there silently, pretending to be asleep. We saw the corridor light go on, then, the very next second, the door opened, and Miss Moreno, the Spanish girls' teacher, looked in. She said something in

Spanish, which was probably "Are you asleep?" and then, when nobody answered, she went out.

We all sat up, breathing huge sighs of relief. But that didn't last long because the next moment we heard Mrs Weaver's voice outside the door. We nearly died.

"Yes, I'm sure I heard someone moving around too," Mrs Weaver was saying. "Have you checked up on all your kids?"

"Not all of them," Miss Moreno said. "I will go and look at the rest now."

"Well, I'd better go and see if mine are all present and correct too," Mrs Weaver said grimly, and we all gasped. Now we were *really* in for it.

"What're we going to do?" Fliss moaned. "Mrs Weaver'll see we're not in our rooms!"

"She might not notice," Lyndz said hopefully.

"Maybe we ought to try and make it back," Rosie suggested.

"Oh yeah, and run slap-bang into Mrs Weaver as soon as we put one foot outside the door!" Kenny pointed out. "We're better off waiting here."

"We could pretend we'd just gone to the loo or something," I said.

"What, all five of us?" Rosie raised her eyebrows. "She'd never swallow that!"

We couldn't decide what to do, so we just stayed where we were, and waited. After a couple of minutes, Mrs Weaver and Miss Moreno came back down the corridor, and we strained our ears to hear what they were saying.

"Well, I can't understand it." Mrs Weaver spoke first. "I know I heard something. But all my pupils are safely tucked up in bed."

That floored us. *We* weren't in bed – well, not in our own beds anyway – but Mrs Weaver didn't seem to have noticed. Anyway, we didn't much care – it looked like we'd got away with it!

We waited for about fifteen minutes to let the teachers get back to sleep again, then we made a break for it. There wasn't much point in letting off the stinkbomb with no one there, so it had all been a waste of time really. *And* we were lucky we hadn't got rumbled by Mrs W...

"Let's get out of here!" Kenny said to our relief, flicking off the corridor light again.

"Can't we keep the lights on?" Fliss wailed.

"No way!" Kenny retorted. "If Mrs Weaver busts us, at least we've got a fighting chance of getting away in the dark!"

We set off. We were so nervous about not making a sound, we were even trying not to *breathe*.

As we inched our way along the corridor wall, I put my hand out, feeling for the corner, which I knew was coming up soon.

And I nearly passed out with shock when my hand touched someone else's fingers...

CHAPTER TEN

I don't know how I stopped myself from screaming, but I did. And if you've ever bumped into someone in the dark unexpectedly and felt their *flesh*, you'll know just how scary it is. I froze right there, but the others kept on coming and bumped into me.

"What's going on?" Fliss squealed.

I groped around for the nearest light switch and turned it on. There in front of us were the Spanish girls – Pilar at the front, with Maria and Isabella behind her and the twins at the back.

"What are *you* doing here?" Pilar and I said furiously right at the same moment.

None of us knew what to say. We didn't know whether to be relieved it wasn't one of our teachers, or annoyed that it was them, so we all stood there looking stupidly at each other, and shuffling our feet.

"We've – er – just been to the bathroom," Rosie said weakly.

"You go the wrong way then," said Maria, jerking a thumb over her shoulder. "The bathroom is this way."

"Well, where've *you* been?" Kenny shot back. "I bet you went to our rooms to play a trick on us!"

The Spanish girls looked embarrassed.

"What a shame we weren't there then!" Fliss said triumphantly.

"So, where were you?" Maria asked suspiciously. "I think *you* also try to play a trick on *us*!"

This time it was our turn to look embarrassed.

"We must've passed each other in the

corridor!" I said. "Did you hiccup?"

Elena turned pink. "I do that."

"She hiccup all the time!" Maria explained.

"That sounds just like someone I know!" I glanced at Lyndz. "Anyway, we saved your necks when your teacher came in to check on you, 'cos we were in your beds, pretending to be you!"

"*So*?" said Pilar. "Your teacher come to check on *you* also – and we did same thing!"

"You mean, you were in *our* beds and we were in *yours*?" Fliss gasped.

"What about Alana Banana?" I asked. "Didn't she notice?"

"You mean that girl who sound like a pig?" Maria grinned. "No, she not wake up!"

We all looked at each other. Then we started to giggle. The Spanish girls *were* just like us, after all. Suddenly our big war seemed really stupid and how we had all been creeping around each other's rooms seemed really funny. We tried to stop laughing, but we couldn't.

"You come to our room!" Maria mouthed

at us, so we all hurried silently back down the corridor to their bedroom. Once we were inside, though, we all collapsed onto the beds, shaking with laughter.

"I can't believe Alana Banana didn't notice what was going on!" Kenny was lying on Maria's bed, stuffing a corner of the duvet into her mouth to muffle her giggles. "That girl's so dozy, she'd forget her own name!"

"Is this her real name – Alana Banana?" Anna said in a serious voice.

That cracked the Sleepover Club up.

"Why do you laugh?" Anna said, looking a bit prickly like Rosie does sometimes.

So we quickly explained about the M&Ms, and about Alana. If I was a beanpole like Pilar, and Kenny and Maria were totally alike, and Lyndz and Elena both got the hiccups, then Anna was definitely a bit like Rosie!

"So, what trick you try to play on us?" Maria asked curiously.

Kenny pulled the box of stinkbombs out of the pocket of her pyjamas, and held it up.

"And us!" said Maria, and she did exactly the same thing.

"Maybe *that* would have woken Alana Banana up!" Rosie suggested, and set us all off laughing again.

When we'd finally stopped giggling, we sat there looking at each other in silence. It felt a bit weird. I mean, we'd been enemies for the last three days, and now here we were, getting on like great mates.

"I very sorry I say English football teams are not good," Maria said suddenly.

"And I'm sorry I thought you'd taken my bag!" Kenny added immediately.

"I'm sorry I tipped you off your surfboard," Lyndz said to Elena.

"And I am sorry we throw your clothes in the tree," Pilar told us.

"Right, so we're all sorry about *everything*," I said. "Let's talk about something else now!"

"You want some Coca-Cola?" Pilar took some cans out of her bedside locker. "We have crisps also."

"Hey, this is just like being at a sleepover!"

Rosie said.

"Sleep over? What is this?" Anna asked, looking interested.

"You know. *Dormir sobre*," I said. "At least I think that's what they're called in Spanish."

"Ah, you mean like a pyjama party," laughed Pilar. "We have them sometimes too."

I nodded. "Yeah, kind of, but we have *special* ones. We're the Sleepover Club!"

"I do not understand. What is that?" Maria asked.

"It's a secret, but we could tell you a bit about it, if you really wanted to know…" I glanced at Rosie, Kenny, Fliss and Lyndz, and they all nodded.

So I told them about how the Sleepover Club had started, and they were really into all that. Then I told them about our sleepover song and our membership cards and the midnight feasts. We don't usually go round telling everyone our secrets, but they promised they wouldn't breathe a word about it to anyone. So then we started telling them about some of the adventures we'd had during our sleepovers, and soon we were all crying with laughter.

"What do you say? Will *we* have one of these Sleepover Clubs?" Pilar said, looking at Maria, Elena, Anna and Isabella.

"Yeah, why don't you?" Kenny said eagerly. "We'll help you to organise it!"

"Hey, why don't we have one of our sleepovers right now?" I suggested. "Then we can show you exactly what we do!"

Everyone thought that was a great idea, so we all got into the beds, the Spanish girls at the tops, and the Sleepover Club at the bottoms. We finished off the crisps and the Coca-Cola, and then Maria gave everyone some chocolate. We started off by telling jokes, and then they taught us some Spanish. After that, we told horror stories. Maria was just as good at that as Kenny was, and between them they nearly frightened Fliss and Isabella to death.

Then we showed them some of the dance routines we'd worked out, and they showed us how to flamenco. We had a brilliant time, and it was nearly three o'clock in the morning before we all started yawning.

"I think Sleepover Club is fantastic idea!" Isabella said sleepily.

"So do you think you'll start one yourselves?" I asked.

The Spanish girls nodded.

"Tomorrow you are going to the beach, yes?" Pilar asked. "If you like, we play volleyball together?"

"You bet!" Kenny said eagerly. "See you in the morning!"

So everything turned out fine in the end. We spent the rest of the week going round with Pilar, Maria, Elena and the others, and guess what? We had a sleepover every night – yeah, *every night*! That was a bit of a record even for us!

On the last night we had a really special sleepover. The teachers were having a party themselves and they'd agreed that just this once we could go into each other's rooms.

So, because we could make as much noise as we liked, we showed the Spanish girls how to play all our International Gladiators games.

We'd had such a good time in Spain, I didn't really want to go home. But in another way, I did. You know what it's like – all your mum and dad do is nag nag nag when you're at home, then when you go away, you can't wait to see them again! And I was *really* missing Pepsi.

"Back home to boring old Cuddington!" Kenny sighed, as we climbed onto the minibus. "I wish we could've stayed for another week!"

"Me too," Fliss said, waving at Pilar and the others who'd come to see us off.

"It's a shame we didn't have long to get to know them," Rosie said gloomily, waving too. "D'you realise we'll probably never see them again in the whole of our lives?"

That made us all feel pretty gruesome.

"Everyone here?" Mrs Weaver hurried down the bus with her clipboard, checking us off one by one. "Right, I think we're just about ready to leave."

We all stood up and opened the windows.

"'BYE!" we yelled. "*Adiós*! Write and tell us about your sleepovers!"

"We will!" they called back, and we all waved until we couldn't see each other any more.

"Have you had a good time?" Mrs Weaver asked us as the minibus headed towards the airport. "I noticed you were getting very friendly with some of the Spanish girls." She smiled. "Well, towards the end of the week, anyway!"

We all turned a bit pink.

"I thought you might like to know that Miss Moreno and I have been talking about making exchange visits between our schools," Mrs Weaver went on. "We'd go to visit their school in Madrid, and they'd come to ours in Cuddington. What do you think?"

We all sat up.

"That sounds excellent, Miss!" Kenny said

eagerly.

"So we'll see them again after all!" Rosie squealed, as Mrs Weaver went back to her seat. "That's brilliant!"

"We'd better start learning Spanish then!" I pulled the dictionary out of my pocket and started flicking through it. "What does…"

The others groaned, and Kenny threw her baseball cap at me.

So that was our trip to Spain! Pretty good, huh? Well, it turned out better than it started, anyway. I guess you're probably thinking "Hey, they didn't get into that much trouble either!" – which makes a change. OK, so we had one sticky episode with Mrs Weaver, but we didn't do too badly, did we?

Wrong!

I *told* Kenny not to put that box of stinkbombs in the bottom of her bag, but she didn't take any notice. I *told* her to be careful when she dropped her bag on the floor in the airport lounge, and dashed off to buy a burger.

Ever smelt a whole box of stinkbombs going off at the same time?

They practically had to evacuate the airport! And Mrs Weaver took her life in her hands, and went sniffing round all the bags, trying to find out who was to blame. She wasn't at all surprised when she found out it was Kenny, but it wouldn't be a sleepover adventure without at least *one* disaster, would it?

See ya!

Sleepover on Friday 13th

Join the Sleepover Club: Frankie, Kenny, Felicity, Rosie and Lyndsey, five girls who just want to have fun – but who always end up in mischief.

The next sleepover is set for a Friday... Friday 13th! Fliss is terrified at the very idea, especially as some scary things seem to have been happening recently. Kenny plans some spooky surprises but, suddenly, everything starts to get out-of-control...

Join the Sleepover girls for their scariest night yet!

0 00 675392 2